AFTER SCHOOL HEROES

MILES MORALES UNTANGLES A WEB

By Terrance Crawford
Illustrated by Dave Bardin

SIMON SPOTLIGHT
NEW YORK LONDON TORONTO SYDNEY NEW DELHI

SIMON SPOTLIGHT
An imprint of Simon & Schuster Children's Publishing Division
1230 Avenue of the Americas, New York, New York 10020
This Simon Spotlight edition August 2024

Simon & Schuster: Celebrating 100 Years of Publishing in 2024
For information about special discounts for bulk purchases, please contact
Simon & Schuster Special Sales at 1-866-506-1949
or business@simonadnschuster.com.
Illustrations by Dave Bardin
Cityscape illustration by Bakal/iStock
Designed by Nicholas Sciacca
Manufactured in the United States of America 0724 LAK
10 9 8 7 6 5 4 3 2 1
This book has been cataloged with the Library of Congress.
ISBN 978-1-6659-5906-3 (hc)
ISBN 978-1-6659-5905-6 (pbk)
ISBN 978-1-6659- 5907-0 (ebook)

CONTENTS

CHAPTER 1:

SPIDER-MAN'S SURPRISE

THWIP!

Strands of webbing burst forth from a trio of nozzles, braiding together into a thick rope and attaching to a nearby rooftop. Miles Morales, aka Spider-Man, wrapped the fibers tightly around his palm and swung in an arc over the city.

"WA-HOOOO!" Miles cheered as he

released the webbing and sailed high into the air, landing on the ledge of a tall building.

Miles pulled his mask from his face and took a deep breath. The city was brimming with life, and Miles had a perfect view of it. This was a familiar spot for him. His dad had grown up on the street below and had taken Miles here to see it many times. Now Miles was working on a digital painting of the entire street for his father's birthday.

But Miles couldn't linger any longer. No matter how beautiful the skyline over Brooklyn looked this time of day, his art class at the Stark Center in New York City would start with or without him there.

Once he was in Manhattan, Miles quickly threw his clothes on over his Spider-Man suit. Sliding down a fire escape, he slung his backpack over his shoulder and stepped out into the crosswalk.

The Stark Center was a community center in the heart of the city, built by the one-and-only Tony Stark and open to any and all kids with a passion for arts, sports, or academics. Miles loved going there. All the equipment was high-tech, state-of-the-art, and top-of-the-line.

Miles rushed through the Stark Center, humming along to the music blaring through his headphones. He quickly rounded a corner and collided with someone. Miles dropped his backpack. Its contents spilled across the floor. He scrambled to pick everything up and reached for the other person's drumsticks.

"You okay, Miles?" she asked.

"Hey, Gwen!" Miles replied.

Gwen Stacy held out a photo that had fallen out of his bag. Miles took it gently, handing her the drumsticks in return.

"Thanks," said Miles. "This is a photo of my dad's childhood street. I thought it might be a nice birthday gift if I made a digital painting of it for him."

"Cool. I'd love to see your work sometime," Gwen said.

"I've actually got the street scene here," Miles exclaimed, eager to show off his painting. "Come into the art room for a moment. I still prefer to paint by hand, but I can't knock Tony Stark's taste in computer programs."

"Look here," Miles said. Gwen peered down at his monitor.

"Uh-oh. I don't know how this happened," Miles said, clicking on different folders.

"What's wrong?" Gwen asked.

"This sort of looks like my painting," Miles said. "But it's a copy . . . it's not quite right. Oh wait . . . here's my painting." Miles tried to open up a file, but when he did, both paintings—his original

work and the copy—disappeared! "This computer must have some kind of virus. Or it was hacked!" He frantically searched through all his files, then rebooted the computer. "I can't believe this."

"That is no fun," Gwen sympathized. "But you have a backup, right?"

"No!" Miles said, running a hand through his hair in frustration. "I realized the other day I hadn't made a backup and was planning to do that today."

"Oh, Miles, I'm so sorry," Gwen said. "That's horrible. But I've got to head to my music class now or I'll be late."

"What are you doing in music class?" Miles asked as he waited for the computer to boot back up.

"I'm going to perform a drum solo!" Gwen replied. "One of my friends in class wrote an original song, and she thought it could use a little of my pizzazz. I'll see you soon. I hope you find your files."

CHAPTER 2:

SHURI IS ON THE WAY

Gwen was right; she would see Miles soon. It had barely been ten minutes before she stormed back into the art room. "Something's going on, and we have to figure it out fast," she said. "I was all set to start banging out my drum solo. But when my friend went to play her new song on the computer, all her original music was gone.

That sounds like what happened to you, right?"

"It does!" agreed Miles. He tried to remain calm but now he was panicking. *What else is missing?* he wondered. Suddenly, he had an idea. Pulling up the faculty directory on his phone, Miles quickly found a listing for the IT department to let them know about

the problem going on in the system, and dashed off a message.

Hello, the email read. *My name is Miles Morales, and I'm an art student here at the Stark Center. There's some weird stuff going on with the tech today. Files are disappearing, in the art and music departments and who knows where else. Can you please send someone to look into this?*

Miles put his phone down and it instantly chirped in response. Miles turned to Gwen in shock.

"It's from Tony Stark!" he shouted. He read Mr. Stark's response to Gwen.

"I can't believe you received an email from Iron Man!" Gwen exclaimed. "I saw Tony Stark on TV the other night. He said he was making the Iron Man suit more powerful."

"I'm glad King T'Challa's presentation is tomorrow," Miles said. "Shuri can't get here soon enough. We need to find this hacker—and fast!"

CHAPTER 3:

SOLVING A MYSTERY

The next day the Stark Center was buzzing with people excited to see the king of Wakanda's presentation. Miles managed to catch a glimpse of King T'Challa as he entered the building. There was a young woman walking in step with him, her face buried in some sort of tech tablet.

As the lights dimmed in the auditorium, King T'Challa introduced himself and his sister, the young woman with the tablet.

"Hello, students of the Stark Center!" The king's voice boomed across the audience. "My name is T'Challa, and I am the king of Wakanda. Tony Stark has invited me here today to share some of our nation's cutting-edge technology with you. This presentation would not be possible without the talents of my younger sister, Shuri." Shuri gave a half-interested wave to the audience, still deeply engrossed in her work.

After King T'Challa finished speaking, Gwen and Miles lingered in the back of the room waiting for the crowd to thin out.

"There are a lot of ways to hack into a computer," Gwen said. "It could be anyone, from anywhere."

Miles agreed. "I wish I knew more about computer tech," he said. "I'm sure there's a way to figure out everyone who's logging on to the Stark system."

"Did someone say 'computer tech'?" came a chipper voice behind them. Off the light of Shuri's tablet, Miles could see that her dark eyes were sparkling. "Tony Stark told my brother all about your dilemma, and my brother told me," Shuri began. "I am *so* excited to help solve a mystery!"

Gwen and Miles introduced themselves to Shuri. Gwen was sorry she couldn't stay. "I've got to run to my drum lesson," she said. "While I'm there, I'll check to see if any other files have gone missing in the music department. Good luck, and let me know what you find out!"

Miles brought Shuri to the empty art room. She sat at Miles's computer station and started clicking away. After quite a bit of coding, analyzing data, and watching ones and zeroes darting across the screen, Shuri let out a long sigh. "I have good news and bad news," she said as she spun her chair to face Miles.

Miles leaned in over the computer, trying to decipher the codes on the screen. "What's the good news?"

"I was able to pull a location for our mysterious hacker."

"Okay . . . ," Miles said, steeling himself for part two of her statement. "What's the bad news?"

"The hacker is inside the Stark Center!"

!!!
HELLO
Miles

CHAPTER 4:

WEB DEVELOPMENT

"Why would someone want to hack the Stark Center files?" Shuri mused out loud. "What might they be hoping to find here?"

Shuri's questions were valid. Even though Miles and the other kids loved it here, he didn't see any particular value in stealing artwork and music from a community center. So what could the hacker

be looking for? The answer hit Miles hard. "The Iron Man suit!" he exclaimed. "It's the most valuable thing Tony owns. The hacker might think Tony has the plans for the suit on the Stark Center server."

Shuri nodded. "Yes! The hacker isn't trying to steal children's art projects. The hacker thinks they can find a real prize.

Where better to hide your jewels than amongst the muck!" Shuri looked up from her tablet sheepishly. "No offense."

Miles shrugged. "Digital painting isn't my best work. But this will be. Let's give the hacker what they're looking for." He created a brand-new folder and labeled it IRON MAN SUIT INSTRUCTIONS. With Shuri's help, Miles wrote out detailed fake

instructions on how to build the Iron Man suit—materials needed, assembly directions, even the length of all the nuts and bolts. It wasn't long before the pair had a convincing set of Iron Man blueprints across several files.

"Now what?" Miles asked.

"Now we wait," Shuri replied.

A few minutes later when Shuri clicked on their file folder, it had been cleaned out from top to bottom. Their trap had worked!

Shuri double-checked the location she found for the hacker and confirmed that it was in the building. "What do you say we stop by and pay the hacker a visit?"

Just as Miles was about to agree, he felt a familiar buzzing at the base of his skull. His Spidey-Sense was tingling. It was a feeling that meant that danger was near. "Uhhh, yes," he told Shuri. "We should definitely do that! I just have to run a quick errand for my mom first." Miles grabbed his backpack and raced out of the art room. "You know how parents are . . . ," he said lamely, letting the door slam behind him.

Bursting into a janitor's closet, he locked the door behind him, tugged off his hoodie, and changed as quickly as he could in cramped conditions into Spider-Man.

CHAPTER 5:

WORLD WIDE WEB

THOOM!

Before Shuri could wonder what was going on with Miles, the art room door flew open. "Back so soon, Miles?" Shuri asked over her shoulder, not looking up from her tablet.

"WHERE IS HE?" a stranger roared. A man in a trench coat towered over Shuri.

"Where is who?" Shuri asked.

"Iron Man!" the stranger yelled. "His suit specs were incomplete! So, I'm here to copy that suit from him, piece by piece!"

It was the Stark Center's hacker!

Where is Miles? Shuri wondered.

Hopefully, whatever errand he was running wouldn't take him too long. In the meantime, she was going to have to deal with this villain by herself. At the moment he was kicking a closet door off its hinges, yelling, "Where are you, Iron Man?"

Shuri quickly typed a series of commands into her tablet, and the device projected a hologram of Tony Stark in his Iron Man suit.

The stranger caught sight of the hologram and shouted gleefully, "There you are! Now I will finally have Iron Man's powers!"

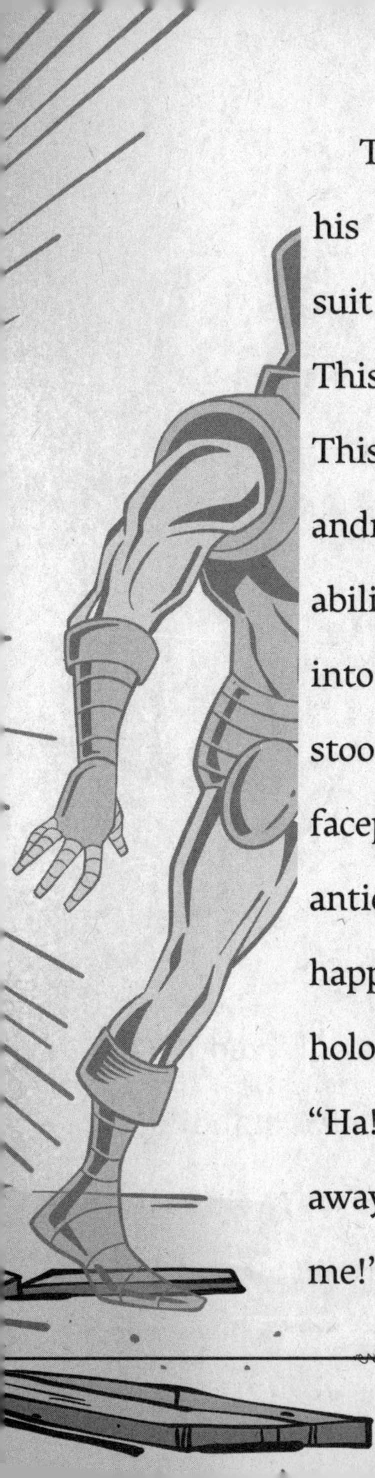

The stranger ripped off his coat, revealing a green suit and robotic features. This was no regular hacker. This was Super-Adaptoid, an android designed to copy the abilities of anyone he came into close contact with. He stood close to the hologram, faceplate lighting up with anticipation, but nothing happened. Shuri moved the hologram toward the door.

"Ha! Are you trying to get away? Come back and fight me!" he yelled at Iron Man.

"He won't fight you, but I will," someone said. The Adaptoid turned and was greeted by the amazing Spider-Man! He was standing on the ceiling, which was the only way that he could look at Super-Adaptoid face-to-face.

The Adaptoid moved closer and narrowed his eyes at Spider-Man. Then he smiled. “You may not be Iron Man,” he said, “but Spider-Man will make an excellent consolation prize!”

Spider-Man created a web to distract Super-Adaptoid while he figured out his next move. But when he looked at the android, his eyes widened in amazement. Super-Adaptoid was now a green Spider-Man, and was gleefully shooting webs all over the room.

"He's able to mimic your powers," Shuri told Spider-Man as she created more holograms, this time of the Wakandan royal guard—the Dora Milaje. She wanted the Adaptoid to think they had an army ready to fight him. "Fascinating!"

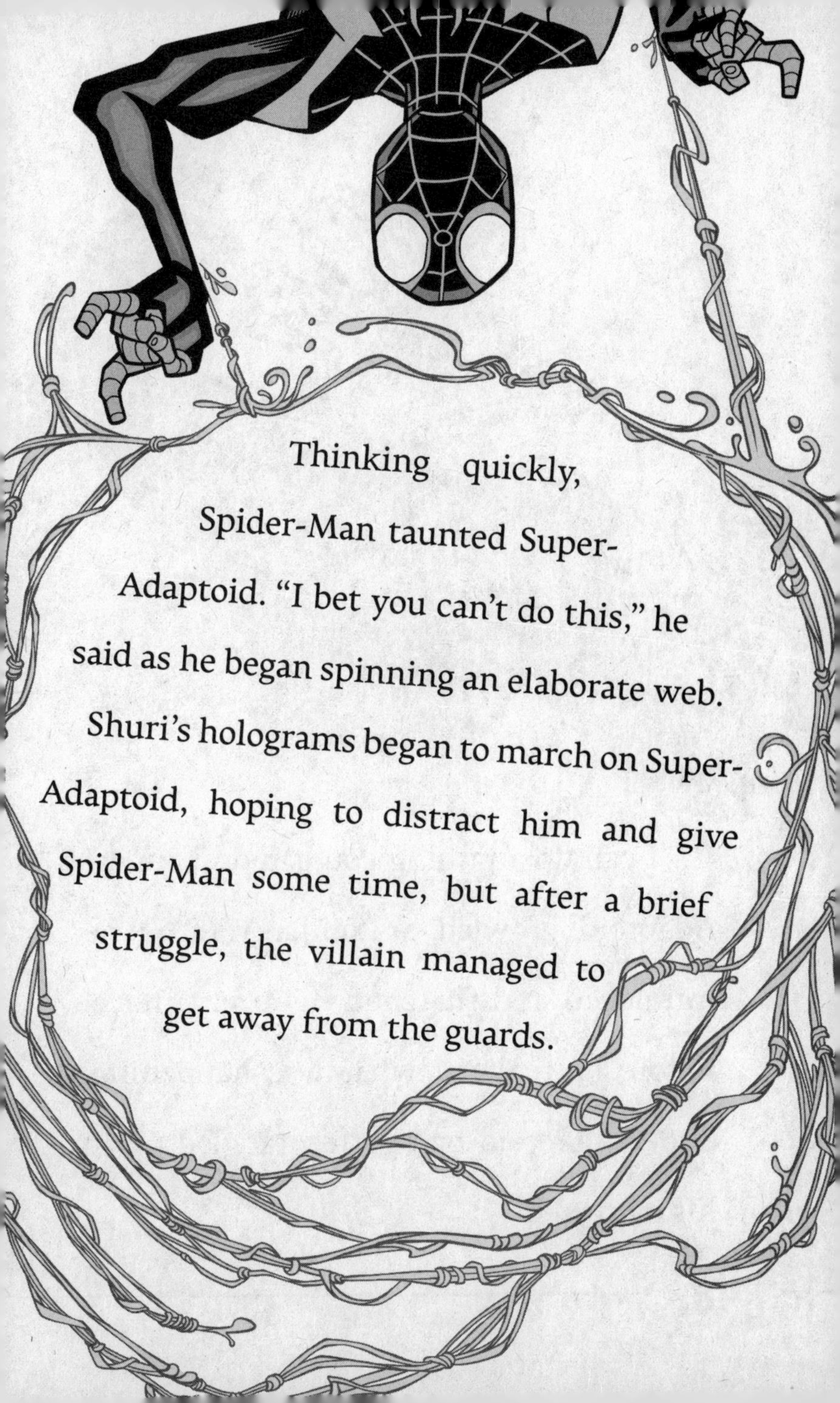

Thinking quickly, Spider-Man taunted Super-Adaptoid. “I bet you can’t do this,” he said as he began spinning an elaborate web. Shuri’s holograms began to march on Super-Adaptoid, hoping to distract him and give Spider-Man some time, but after a brief struggle, the villain managed to get away from the guards.

"I can do anything you can do," Super-Adaptoid growled at Spider-Man as he mimicked and matched his every move. Before he realized what was happening, Super-Adaptoid had gotten tangled up in his own web!

"My plan worked!" Spider-Man shouted happily. "You may be able to imitate me, but you couldn't figure out that this was a trap!" Then Spider-Man shot a blinding blur of web over Super-Adaptoid's visual sensors so the robot couldn't see his next move, which was to quickly maneuver himself out of his own web.

"Nice work, Spider-Man," Shuri cheered as Super-Adaptoid struggled helplessly to get out of his self-made cocoon.

“Tell Mr. Stark we’ve caught the hacker,” Spider-Man said. “And tell him he doesn’t have to rush back—this guy’s not going anywhere.” Spider-Man knocked on Super-Adaptoid’s metal-plated chest, waved goodbye to Shuri, and leapt up onto the ceiling. Giving Shuri a Wakandan salute, he then disappeared out of the window.

What an afternoon in New York City this has turned out to be! Shuri thought.

Shuri's holograms dispersed just as Miles burst back in through the door in his street clothes. "Sorry! My errand took longer than I expected," he said. He saw Super-Adaptoid struggling in the corner. "Um . . . what happened here?" he asked.

Shuri could barely contain her excitement. "You won't believe it!" she exclaimed. "Super-Adaptoid was the hacker. He came to fight

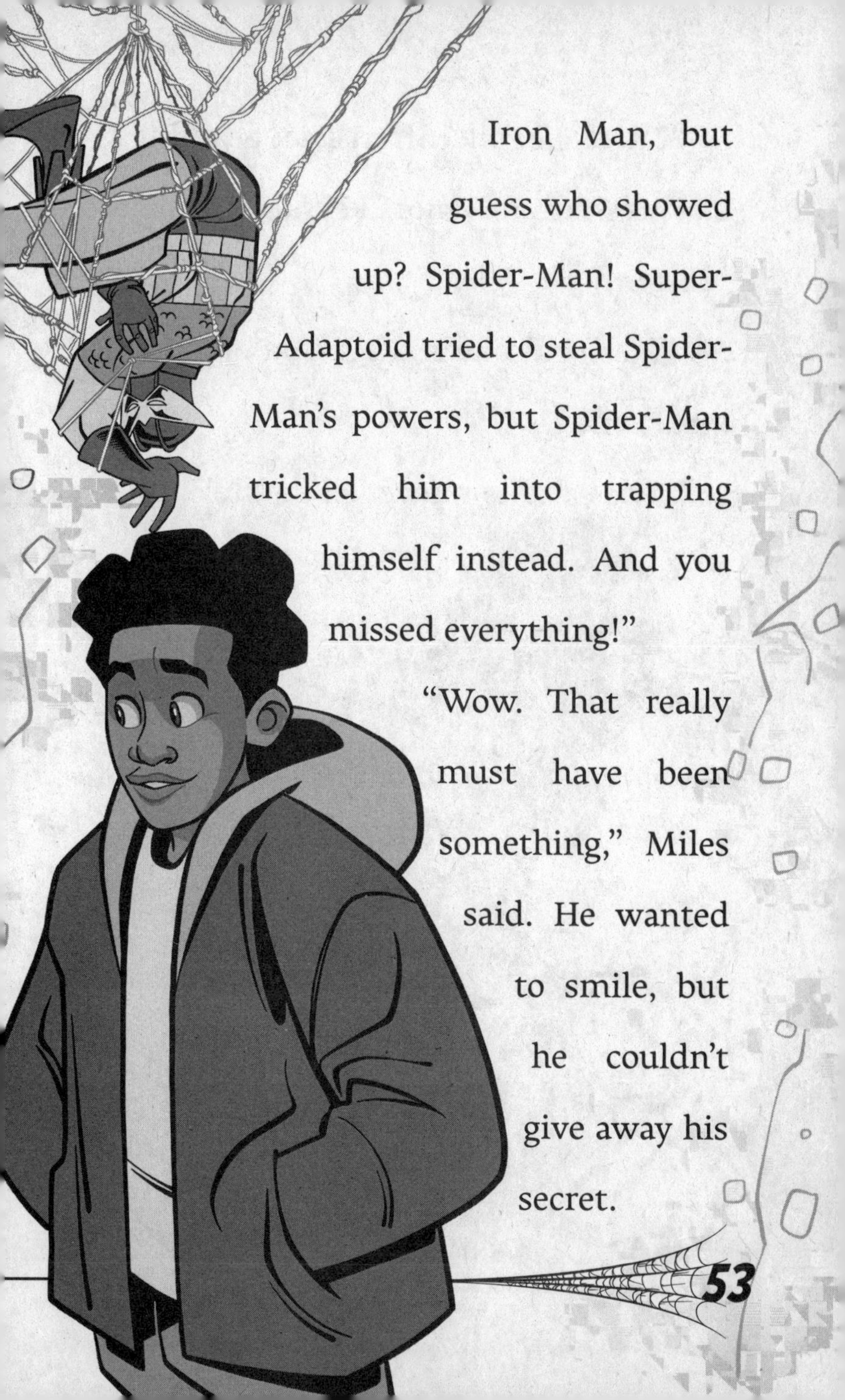

Iron Man, but guess who showed up? Spider-Man! Super-Adaptoid tried to steal Spider-Man's powers, but Spider-Man tricked him into trapping himself instead. And you missed everything!"

"Wow. That really must have been something," Miles said. He wanted to smile, but he couldn't give away his secret.

"That's not all!" Shuri said, beaming as she pressed a few more keys on her tablet. "Listen!"

Miles could hear the sound of a guitar strumming.

"I was able to recover all the stolen files,

including the original song Gwen's friend wrote," Shuri said proudly.

Miles didn't want to get ahead of himself, but he felt a spark of hope. "All the files?" he asked.

Shuri showed Miles her tablet. There was the digital painting he'd made for his dad! His files were safe, just the way he had left them. "Thank you, Shuri. I couldn't have done it without you." Miles extended his arms for a hug. "I hope things are calmer next time you come to visit the Stark Center."

"Are you kidding?" Shuri said. "I was able to fix Tony Stark's tech, retrieve your lost artwork, and see Spider-Man in action! It was the best afternoon ever!"

You don't need to be a superhero to read a sneak peek of our next Marvel After-School Heroes book, ***GHOST-SPIDER'S UNBREAKABLE MISSION!***

GREAT EGGSPECTATIONS

Gwen Stacy stared at the egg on her desk. Every student in Mr. Anzelone's science class had one. But what did her teacher want them to do with it? Gwen raised her hand.

"Thanks for the present, Mr. A," she said. "But next time how about a gift card?"

Mr. Anzelone laughed. "Sorry, Gwen.

This is your homework. Over the weekend I would like each of you to take care of your egg. You can talk to it, take it on walks—"

"Watch a movie with it?" joked Gwen's classmate Amir.

"Whatever you want," Mr. Anzelone replied. "But remember, eggs are fragile. They can easily break. Your assignment is to bring the egg back on Monday in one piece. Show me how responsible you can be by caring for something so delicate."

The bell rang. "Your eggs are depending on you!" Mr. Anzelone said. "Class dismissed."

Gwen packed up her backpack. She spoke to her egg. "Don't worry about a thing, little eggy," she said, "because you hit the babysitting jackpot. I'm probably the most responsible kid in this class. But it's not just because I know not to toss you in the air." Gwen lowered her voice to a whisper. "It's because I'm a super hero."